D0468294

Copyright of The Islamic Foundation. 2003 / 1424 AH.
Third Impression 2016 / 1437 H.

ISBN 978-0-86037-338-4

All rights reserved.
No part of this publication may be reproduced, stored in a retrieval
system or transmitted by any means whatsoever without the prior
permission of the copyright owner.

MUSLIM CHILDREN'S LIBRARY

ALLAH THE MAKER SERIES

Allah Gave Me A Tongue To Taste

Author: *Ayesha Jones*
Illustrator & Designer: *Steven Stratford*
Co-ordinator: *Raana Bokhari*

Published by
The Islamic Foundation
Markfield Conference Centre
Ratby Lane, Markfield
Leicester LE67 9SY
United Kingdom
T (01530) 244 944
F (01530) 244946
E i.foundation@islamic-foundation.org.uk

Quran House, PO Box 30611, Nairobi, Kenya

PMB 3193, Kano, Nigeria

Distributed by
Kube Publishing Ltd.
T +44(0)1530 249230
F +44(0)1530 249656
E info@kubepublishing.com

Printed by Imak Ofset, Turkey

British Library Cataloguing in Publication Data

Jones, Ayesha
    Allah Gave me a tongue to taste. - (Allah the maker series)
    1. Taste - Juvenile literature 2. Taste - Religious aspects -
    Islam - Juvenile literature 3. Tongue - Juvenile literature
    4. Tongue - Religious aspects - Islam - Juvenile literature
    I. Title II. Islamic Foundation
    612.8'7

Allah Gave Me
A TONGUE TO TASTE

Ayesha Jones

Illustrated by Stevan Stratford

THE ISLAMIC FOUNDATION

Allah gave me a tongue to taste!

All sorts of food that I like to try.
Delicious food, like apple-pie.

He made for me a tongue to test,
What kinds of flavours I like best.

When I close my eyes and put food
on my tongue,

I can guess what it is –
but I might be wrong!

Tiny taste buds test the things I eat,
They tell me if it's nasty,
or a tasty treat!

Allah gave me a tongue to taste!

Lemons are bitter, not easy to eat,
Sugar is sweet, a welcome treat!

Yoghurt is sour, but not with
fruit in it,
And fruit keeps me well and
healthy and fit.

Salty things are savouries, like chicken and roast,
   One of my favourites is cheese on toast.

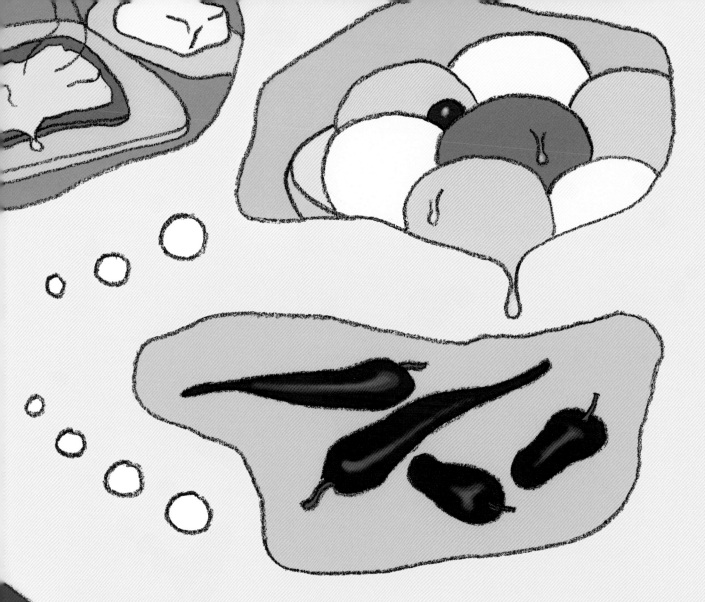

Ice cream is cold, but chillies are hot.
My taste buds decide if I eat it or not.

Cream feels smooth, but biscuits
are crunchy!

I clean my teeth quickly,
when I eat something munchy!

My taste buds tickle when
I drink something fizzy,
I begin to chuckle and feel
quite dizzy!

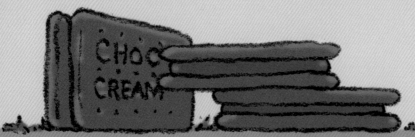

Allah gave me a tongue to taste!

Food is good for us, it helps us to grow,
It makes us healthy, but it's best if
you know

That some foods are good, and some foods are not.

Mummy will know – she'll tell you about that.

My friends all come from different lands,
Some eat with chopsticks, and some eat
with their hands.

Others eat with knives and
forks - as they wish,
But eat up every crumb,
leave nothing in your dish!

I love to eat spaghetti, but
I always start off giggling,
When it slides off my fork,
wriggling and wiggling!

Chicken curry with chapatties makes
a good tasty meal.
You can eat it mild or hot, it
depends on how you feel!

Allah gave me a tongue to taste!

We all know well what we should eat,
All that's halal, including animal meat.

Milk and honey, olives, figs and dates,
Fruits, vegetables, ginger and lush grapes!

All these foods are in Allah's Holy Book,
Let's sit down together and have a look!

That's what the Prophet told us to do,
And to be grateful for what Allah's
given you.

There's no better drink than
pure Zam-Zam,
And dates from the desert ...
yum, yum, yum!

Thank you, O Allah, for providing for me,
Foods in abundance, and such variety!

Tastes that are ...
Scrumptious,
Yummy,
Delightful in my tummy!

I raise my hands,
TO THANK ALLAH!!!

I've finished my meal now,
AL-HAMDULILLAH!!!